TO MY FAMILY

Especially to my Grampa, the creator of BeBa

This book would not have been completed without the love and support of my family, friends, and mentors. Thank you to everyone who made BeBa a reality and took the time to help me. I am so grateful and appreciative.

- Lydia

Text, Design and Compilation © 2006 Laffin Minor Press, LLC
Illustrations © 2006 Stephanie Lostimolo

BeBa™ is a trademark of Laffin Minor Press, LLC

Library of Congress Control Number: 2005908385

ISBN 13: 978-0-9770516-0-1
ISBN 10: 0-9770516-0-9

Graphic design by Jake Lebovic
Printed and bound by Palace Press International in China

First Edition

An Imaginosis Production
imaginosis.com

Please visit the Official BeBa website:

bebastories.com

BeBa
and the CURIOUS CREATURE CATCHERS

Written by **Lydia Griffin**
Illustrated by **Stephanie Lostimolo**

Laffin Minor Press

There once was a little girl named BeBa.
She lived way out in the country with her loving family.

BeBa's mother was an animal doctor,
yet BeBa had her own special way to help animals.

Early one morning, BeBa woke up and saw something large and striped peering in her window.

"What could it be?" BeBa wondered.

"Good morning, I'm BeBa. What's your name?"

"I'm Zilly the Zebroose. The Curious Creature Catchers are after me. Can you help?"

"What's a Zebroose? And what's a Curious Creature Catcher?" BeBa asked.

"My mother was a zebra and my father was a moose," Zilly explained. "And the Curious Creature Catchers are horrible! They trap animals that are different and sell them to mean people."

"That's not right at all," said BeBa. "I'd be happy to help you, but first I need to eat breakfast and do my chores. Stay right here. I'll be back in a flash."

Her chores done, BeBa grabbed her little red backpack.
She pulled out her soda pop straw and twisted it quickly
while she shouted, "To the forest we go!"

The air around her began to swirl.

Suddenly, BeBa and Zilly were in a forest clearing
and surrounded by animals.

"Are you here to help our friend Zilly?" a fox asked.

"Hmmmm. I have an idea," said BeBa.
"We are going to trick the Curious Creature Catchers.
If that doesn't work, we'll try Plan B.
My father says to always have a Plan B."

BeBa reached into her little red backpack and
pulled out a paint can and a brush.

Soon the bears were purple and the raccoons were blue
and the beaver was yellow and the elk was orange.
The fox was covered with polka dots.

When BeBa was done, each animal stood out colorful, bright,
and beautiful against the green of the woods.

Zilly no longer looked so different.

Putting her straw to her mouth, BeBa blew with all her might. The air around her began to swirl and suddenly she was the size of a baby mouse. Mr. Cardinal flew down from high above and said, "Hop aboard, BeBa. I'll give you a ride."

BeBa spied the Curious Creature Catchers below the big puffy clouds. "Swoop down, Mr. Cardinal, so I can hear what they're saying."

"Look there...a purple bear. That's curious!" said one Catcher. "GET HIM!" "Look...a polka-dotted possum. That's very curious!" shouted another.

"Forget them!" shouted the Leader of the Catchers. "We need to capture the Zebroose. He's the most curious creature of all!"

The Curious Creature Catchers raced around looking for Zilly. They raced up, down, and all around!

Now that the animals
were colorful and different,
Zilly was much harder to find.

Suddenly, the clouds turned dark
and gray. Drop! Drop! Drop!
It started to rain.

The animals' colors began to wash away.
The forest floor became a rainbow river.

The Curious Creature Catchers were closing in on Zilly.
Something had to be done quickly.

"Looks like it's time for Plan B," said BeBa.

"Thank you, Mr. Cardinal," said BeBa as she hopped off his back. She held her straw to her mouth and blew with all her might. The air around her began to swirl and suddenly she was the size of a giant.

BOOM! A red sneaker landed directly in front of the Catchers. BOOM! Another red sneaker landed next to it and completely blocked their way. BeBa reached down with her huge hand and snatched up the Catchers.

"Zilly is our friend!" BeBa bellowed. "We love him BECAUSE he is different. You will leave him alone. Do you understand me?"

"Yes, ma'am, we do. Please don't EAT us!" cried the quivering Catchers.

"You will leave this forest and never return. Promise?"

"Yes. We promise. We'll never come back."

"Good," BeBa said as she tossed the Curious Creature Catchers. SPLASH went the first Catcher into the rainbow river. KURPLUNK went the second. The Catchers wiped multi-colored mud from their eyes.

BeBa put her straw to her lips and blew with all her might. The air around her began to swirl and suddenly she was her normal size again.

"Hey, should we catch these Curious Creatures?" laughed one of the elk.

"They sure are funny looking!" giggled the raccoons.

"Yes they are," said BeBa, "but there is no need to capture or make fun of things that are different."

BeBa and the animals smiled as the Curious Creature Catchers scrambled away.

"How can we ever thank you, BeBa?" asked Zilly.

"Parties are always good," said a bear.

"Thanks so much, but I need to get home," BeBa said.
"It was great to meet you Zilly.
Come visit me anytime."

"I will," said Zilly as BeBa gave him a big hug.

For the last time, BeBa pulled out her straw. She twisted it
quickly while she shouted, "To my home I go!" The air around
her began to swirl and suddenly she was walking down
her long driveway just in time for dinner.

BeBa sank into her chair at the dining room table. She looked down at her overalls. They were covered with rainbow paint.

"BeBa, did you have a busy day?" her mother asked.

BeBa yawned. "Yes, and now I'm a little sleepy."

"I'll tuck you in after dinner. You need a good night's sleep. You never know what adventures tomorrow will bring."

THE END